THE REAL GHOSTBUSTERS™

JANINE'S GENIE

When a client offers the Ghostbusters the pick of his belongings instead of payment, Janine chooses a ridiculous, old brass oil-lamp and unleashes a load of trouble on to town, in the shape of a lampful of ghosts and ghouls.

Ghostbusters are here to save the world!

The first title in the real Ghostbuster™ Series

The Ghostbusters' Headquarters

THE REAL GHOSTBUSTERS™

JANINE'S GENIE

novelisation by
Kenneth Harper

Illustrated by Jon Miller

KNIGHT BOOKS
Hodder and Stoughton

First published by Knight Books 1988

British Library C.I.P.

Harper, Kenneth, *1940–*
  Janine's genie.—(The real ghostbusters).
  Rn: Keith Miles I. Title II. Miller, Jon, *1947–* III. Series
  823'.914[J] PZ7

  ISBN 0-340-42126-6

Printed and bound in Great Britain for Hodder and Stoughton Paperbacks, a division of Hodder and Stoughton Limited, Mill Road, Dunton Green, Sevenoaks, Kent TN13 2YA (Editorial Office: 47 Bedford Square, London WC1B 3DP) by Cox and Wyman Limited, Reading, Berks. Photoset by Rowland Phototypesetting Limited, Bury St Edmunds, Suffolk.

1

Waiting for a Call

Peace reigned. In the old fire station that the Ghostbusters used as their headquarters, everything was quiet and untroubled. They were waiting around for their next case. It was eerie. The Ghostbusters were without a ghost, waiting for their next call.

Egon Spengler was up on the top floor of the building. He was tall, fair-haired and eccentric, and was completely dedicated to science. Whenever there was a lull in ghostbusting, he could be found pottering away in the laboratory. It was a labyrinth of wires, cables, screens, lights and consoles. Egon was the inventor of all the complicated gadgetry and no one else had a clue how it worked!

His colleagues were down on the first floor. They were trying to relax in the large, cluttered area that was a kitchen, dining-room and lounge all rolled into one. It was the ideal place to put your feet up and take it easy, but Dr Peter Venkman could do neither. He could not put

5

his feet up because the low table opposite him was covered in unwashed coffee cups. And he couldn't relax because he was keeping a wary eye on Slimer.

Peter was the showman among the Ghostbusters. He was hip, sharp-witted and a bit of a rascal. When things went wrong – and they often did – Peter was always the first to confront the unknown with his ready smile and his smooth tongue. If Egon was the Brain, Peter was definitely the Mouth.

The Ghostbusters had a major problem.

Slimer.

'Glug-glug. Schhh-lim-er!'

He was the green ghostie who slimed Peter on his first day and had never really been forgiven. A huge, shapeless blob of ectoplasm, Slimer was a bundle of contradictions, a ghost who lived with people whose job it was to bust ghosts! He could only speak half-formed words and gibberish, but he got his message across somehow. He really wanted to be loved by people in the real world – and by Peter, in particular. It was not easy.

'Slimer!' warned Peter.

'Glug-glug-glug.'

'Don't you *dare*!'

Slimer could not stop eating. Unless they watched him carefully, he would devour the entire contents of the fridge. Peter was guarding the big, juicy water-melon that stood on the table. Slimer could not take his eyes off it. Once he got his claws on the melon, it would vanish in seconds.

'Hands off!' said Peter firmly.

6

'Glug-glug-glug.'

'That melon is mine.'

Peter kept him at bay with a stern glare. Slimer grinned sheepishly, showing off his massive teeth and tongue.

Ray Stantz took no notice of him. He was reading a book on the sofa. Nobody knew as much about Weird Things and their history as Ray. He loved it all with the innocent joy of a child.

Most people would flee in the face of supernatural danger. Not Ray Stantz. He would stand in awe before it, proclaiming the scientific importance of the event. Ray was also the mechanic of the team and he built the fantastic devices that Egon dreamed up. Whenever the Ghostbusters needed a skilled pair of hands, Ray was there.

'Glug-glug-glug.'

'*No*, Slimer!' cautioned Peter.

But the melon was very tempting.

On the ground floor of the building was the reception area. It had desks, filing cabinets, telephones, wall charts and a slightly old-fashioned air about it. The reception area was the private domain of Janine Melnitz and it was there that the action began.

Janine was an attractive, scatty-looking girl with glasses on the end of her nose, and she was highly efficient. Nothing ever rattled her and she could be sarcastic to her colleagues about their work. Janine spent a lot of time shaking her head in disbelief at the difficulties in which the Ghostbusters landed themselves.

She was much more than simply a typist. Janine Melnitz was at the centre of operations, looking after the team, sending them out on missions, and coping with all their strange ways. She knew that it was the secretaries who really ruled the world. Janine had a crush on Egon Spengler but he was not even aware of it. Apart from ghostbusting, his only interest was collecting spores, moulds and fungus. She could not compete with that.

'Oh, Egon!' she sighed, filing her fingernails. 'If only I was a spore or a fungus! You'd pay attention then. I *need* you.'

'Then here I am.'

'Oh!'

The voice behind her made her drop her nail-file.

Winston Zeddmore had just come into the room.

'Did I hear you say you needed me, Janine?' he asked.

He beamed helpfully. Winston was the vital fourth member of the group and the only one who had his feet firmly on the ground. He showed up one day in search of a job. Any job. They turned him into a Ghostbuster.

Winston did not have the scientific training of the others, but he possessed qualities that they lacked. He was the most direct and practical of the Ghostbusters. For sheer guts, bravery and loyalty, nobody could touch Winston Zeddmore.

'What can I do for you, Janine?' he offered.

'Pick up my nail-file.'

'Oh, sure.'

When Winston had given it to her, he went off upstairs

to join the others. Like them, he was eager for a new case. Janine, meanwhile, lapsed back into thoughts of her beloved.

'Egon! Notice me!'

She began to file her nails again.

Down in the basement was the true heart of the Ghostbusting business. It was there that the ghosts were stored. They were kept in the ecto-containment unit which Egon had designed. It was a huge complex made out of steel. The captured ghosts were deposited in there and held behind an ion grid.

'Wheeeeeeeeeeee!'

They swirled around inside, trying to escape.

'Wooooooooooooo!'

Soon, however, they would be joined by other prisoners.

The Ghostbusters wanted to have a ghost-free city.

There was silence on the top floor where Egon worked on an experiment. There was silence on the first floor where Peter, Ray and Zeddmore relaxed, and where even Slimer sat back for once. And in the basement, there was a ghostly silence.

Janine's nail-file made the only noise in the reception area. Then the telephone rang. She answered it at once.

'Hello? Ghostbusters. Can we help you?'

Seconds later, she reached for the alarm bell.

BRRRING-BRRRING!

The peace was shattered. The Ghostbusters leaped up.

BRRRING-BRRRING! BRRRING-BRRRING!

They rushed to the fireman's pole which ran from the top floor to the ground floor. Diving on to it, they slid down at top speed. Winston. Peter. Ray. And – because he had the furthest to come – Egon. All four of them wore their ghostbusting uniforms.

BRRRING-BRRRING! BRRRING-BRRRING! BRRRING-BRRRING!

The alarm bell continued to alarm them.

'Glug-glug-glug.'

Slimer appeared in the circular opening in the floor above and hovered in mid-air. Peter Venkman looked up at the ghost and wagged a finger at him.

'Remember what I told you, Slimer,' he reminded.

'Glug-glug.'

'Stay away from that water-melon. OK?'

'Sch-lurpp!'

'Promise?' said Peter.

Slimer nodded vigorously and his finger drew a cross-my-heart 'X' on his sticky chest. With the final down-stroke, he accidentally flicked a big blob of ectoslime down through the circular opening. It landed right in the middle of Peter's forehead.

'I had to ask!' said Peter ruefully.

'Glug-glug-glug,' added Slimer apologetically.

Janine was standing behind her desk, holding out the memo sheet on which she had written details of the latest case. As the four Ghostbusters sprinted past her, Ray Stantz grabbed the memo from her. She tried to get their attention.

'Guys? . . . Hey, guys!'

12

But they had run on past. Scowling after them, she put her fingers into her mouth and emitted a long, high-pitched whistle.

The shrill blast popped both lenses of Egon's spectacles, so that they looked like spider's webs. Egon removed the glasses to examine the cracked lenses.

'Whew!' he whistled. 'What a whistle!'

The other Ghostbusters skidded to a halt beside their car. Their fingers were in their ears and their teeth were gritted. They looked back in through the door to the reception area.

'It's not fair!' complained Janine.

'What d'ya mean?' asked Ray.

'I always get stuck at this boring desk while you guys get all the action. I wanna go this time. Pleeeease!'

The four Ghostbusters exchanged glances.

'Well,' said Ray with a shrug. 'Sure – why not?'

'YIPPEE!'

Janine raced over at such speed that she knocked the four of them flying as she sailed past. Leaping into the rear seat of their vehicle, Ecto-I, she slammed the door behind her.

The Ghostbusters lay bruised and sprawled on the ground.

'*That's* why not,' moaned Ray.

They picked themselves up and jumped into Ecto-I.

It was an emergency call and there was no time to lose.

The Ghostbusters were after another ghost!

2

New Lamps for Old

The doors of the old fire station swung open and the vehicle shot out like a rocket. With its siren wailing and its light-bar flashing, it surged through the streets of New York City. Ray Stantz was at the wheel and he drove with daredevil skill. The Ghostbusters did not like to keep a ghost waiting.

Ecto-I was a character in itself. Formerly an ambulance, it had been customized to the strange needs of the team. It was loaded with exotic equipment which might or might not work at any given moment. It was a blaze of noise and colour with a 'no-ghosts' logo on its doors. When it roared off through the streets in search of adventure, everyone turned to look.

Janine sat in the back with mounting excitement.

'Say, this is just great!'

'We haven't got there yet,' observed Peter drily.

'I'm dying to see a real ghost!' she said.

'If you died, you'd *be* a real ghost,' noted Egon seriously.

'Where'd the call come from?' asked Winston.

'On the waterfront,' said Ray.

'Let's burn some rubber,' urged Winston.

The tyres screeched as they skidded around a corner. Ecto-I then sped on to the waterfront district and raced past wharves and warehouses. It came to a jarring halt on a pier.

'Everybody out!' ordered Peter.

The four Ghostbusters were out of the vehicle in a flash, running at full pelt towards a dilapidated warehouse. There was a plaintive yell from the car.

'Hey, guys! Wait up, would ya!'

Janine Melnitz struggled to get out of Ecto-I. Like the others, she was wearing regulation Ghostbuster uniform – except that hers did not fit. Her overalls were far too baggy and her boots were much too big. She clumped her way towards the warehouse.

What slowed her down was the Proton Pack on her back. It was the basic Ghostbuster weapon. It consisted of a portable nuclear accelerator and a particle thrower. Attached to it by a cable was a Proton Gun. Janine had not expected it all to be so heavy.

'Where are you guys?' she called.

She glanced up at the building. Bursts of supernatural light flickered and flashed at all the windows. It was like a gigantic fireworks display.

Janine started to have second thoughts.

'Is it *safe* in there, fellas?'

17

From inside the warehouse came the most bizarre and frightening noises she had ever heard, a mixture of wailing, howling and yowling that made her blood turn cold.

'Yoooooooooooo!'

'Eeeeeeeeeeeee!'

'Wahhhhhhhhhhhh!'

Janine tiptoed to the door and peeped cautiously in.

'Ssssssssssssssss!'

The ghastly, ghostly hiss made her knees knock.

'Uh, guys,' she shouted. 'I'll be in the car if you need me.'

She turned to go but Peter Venkman was too quick for her. He took a firm grip on her arm and yanked her inside the building.

'But *this* is where the action is,' he said.

'Guuuuuuuuuuuuh!'

A large ghost was hovering directly in front of them with a defiant grin. Peter, Winston, Ray and Egon fired their Proton Guns but they were unable to nail him. The ghost swooped down to give Janine another scare.

'Whiiiiiiiiiiiisht!'

She was trembling all over now and she stuttered.

'Wh-what d-do I d-do?'

'Don't be afraid,' said Egon to reassure her.

'I'm not afraid,' she replied. 'I'm t-t-terrified!'

'Blast 'em!' encouraged Winston.

'What?'

'Blast 'em with your gun, Janine!'

'Oh . . . yeah.'

18

Plucking up her courage, she aimed her gun and switched it on, opening fire at the ghosts like a female Rambo. She yelled at the top of her voice.

'Take that, you ectoplasmic slime balls!'

But she could not control her weapon. The kick from the unleashed energy bounced her backwards across the floor on her heels. She landed on Egon's toes and made him hop about in pain on one foot.

'Oww!' he cried.

'Oh, Egon. I'm so sorry!'

As she turned to apologize, the beam from her gun streamed out and almost took off Peter's head. He dived to the ground to avoid a nasty accident.

'Whoa, Janine! Leave my head on my shoulders.'

'What am I doing wrong?' she asked.

'Everything!' groaned Peter.

Winston twisted her shoulders so that she faced the ghost.

'This way, Janine,' he advised.

Her particle beam was now right on target.

'You've hit the jackpot!' said Ray excitedly. 'Hold it there!'

The ghost who had swooped on Janine was now held captive in the beam from her Proton Gun. Try as it might, it could not escape. Ray Stantz worked swiftly. Taking out his portable ecto-trap, he moved it across the floor so that it was beneath the hovering entity. He pressed the switch and the jaws flipped apart.

'Trap open!' he announced. 'Come on down, ghostie.'

The spirit roared and ranted above him.

19

'Nooooo! Go awaaaaaay! I want to be freeeee!'

Janine kept her beam trained on him and slowly brought him down to the trap, which suctioned him in. Ray activated the switch and the trap clanged shut with the spirit inside.

Janine jumped up and down with girlish delight.

'My first ghost!' she shouted. 'I bagged my first ghost. Yeeea-ah!'

Picking himself up off the floor, Peter dusted his sleeves.

'You almost bagged your first ghost*buster* as well!'

Janine turned towards him, not realizing that she was pointing the smoking end of her muzzle directly at him.

'Excuse me?' she said.

'Yiiiiiii!' screamed Peter.

He hit the deck again and covered his head with his hands.

Janine was baffled. She pointed a thumb in his direction.

'Isn't he *ever* serious?' she wondered.

Ray Stantz caught hold of the ecto-trap by its power cord.

'That's the last ghostie,' he said with a smile of congratulation. 'Nice job, gang.'

'Gee, that was FUN!' decided Janine now that it was all over. 'Guess this means, I'm a fully-fledged Ghostbuster, huh?'

'Not quite,' Egon replied.

'Oh.' She was deflated.

'There's a bit more to it than that,' said Peter.

'Is there?'

'Nothing personal, Janine,' added Winston kindly, 'but nobody becomes a Ghostbuster overnight.'

'It takes a lot of practice,' argued Ray.

'Practice . . .?'

Janine was crestfallen. She did not want to have to do it all over again. Being a Ghostbuster was not quite as simple and as exhilarating as she had imagined.

Peter Venkman was now standing beside an old desk that was covered by well-worn books and curling papers. There was a desk blotter, a spike full of yellowing invoices and a desk clerk's bell. Peter jotted some information down on a hand-held notepad, then tore off the sheet of paper and held it high. He gave the bell a bash with his other fist.

'PING!'

A grizzled old grandpa poked his head up from behind the desk and Peter almost jumped out of his skin.

'Aghhhhhh!'

'You look as if you've seen a ghost, Peter,' noted Egon.

Dressed in sleeve bands, a green celluloid visor and wire-rimmed spectacles, the old man was clearly more shaken than Peter. Trembling violently, he came out from behind the desk to face them. Peter handed him the slip of paper.

'Bill time!' he cooed.

'S-sorry, Ghostbusters . . .'

'Why?'

'I d-d-don't have any money.'

'*Now* he tells us!' complained Peter.

The old man gestured around the warehouse.

'All I have is these memories I've collected over the years. These keepsakes and souvenirs are very dear to me.'

The Ghostbusters gazed around at the piles of junk that lay under a thick covering of dust and cobwebs. Nothing in the place seemed to be worth a penny.

The old man gave them a toothless grin.

'Y-you're welcome to take anything you want.'

'Who wants dust?' murmured Ray.

'What a dump!' agreed Peter.

'I guess this is a freebie,' said Winston.

'We must put it down to experience,' added Egon.

If the others were disappointed with the offer, Janine was not. Diving forward, she grabbed the old man's hand and shook it so vigorously that he was quite jangled.

'Thanks!' she said. 'We'd love to!'

'We would?' asked Winston.

'Of course. We might find something really valuable.'

'Such as?' he pressed.

'Who knows? Buried treasure, maybe.'

'In *that* muck heap?' demanded Peter sceptically.

But Janine was not dismayed. She had faith that she would find something very special if only she searched carefully enough. She looked around and smacked her hands together purposefully.

'Leave this to me, guys!'

They watched in admiration as she pitched into her

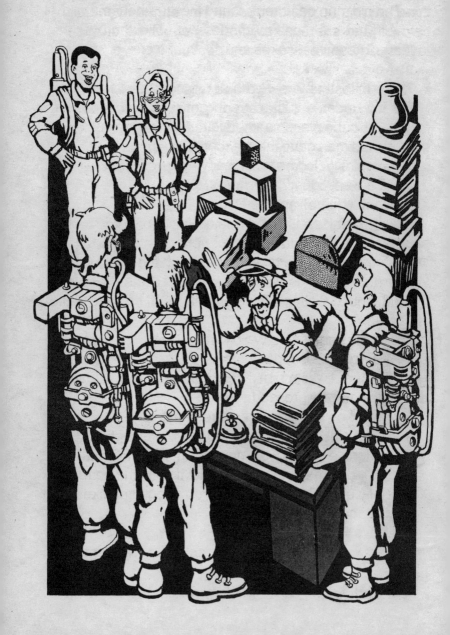

task. Janine was thorough. She went through every-thing, stirring up clouds of dust. Her efforts eventually paid off and she emerged in triumph with a strange-looking object in her hands.

'I've got it,' she said. 'Look!'

They did. But all they could do was to laugh at her.

It was a battered, old, brass oil-lamp that looked as if it might once have belonged to Aladdin. Ugly and tar-nished, it seemed to have nothing in its favour.

'Janine,' said Egon, snickering. 'Why would you want such an eyesore?'

She was insulted and stood on her dignity.

'Go ahead and laugh, Quiche-eaters!' she retorted. '*I* think this lamp is beautiful.'

The mocking laughter continued. Peter nudged Winston.

'Better not rub it, Janine,' said Peter.

'Why not?'

'A genie might pop out. A Janeenie!'

The Ghostbusters shook with mirth.

But the laugh would soon be on them.

3

Water-melon Missiles

Back at Ghostbuster headquarters, Slimer was in his seventh heaven. He had pounced on the water-melon. It was delicious. Sitting in the kitchen area on the first floor, he held a slice of melon and took a big, guzzling bite out of it. After chewing it noisily for a few seconds, he swallowed it with a gulp then turned his head to spit out the seeds. They went into a bin that was already full of melon rind.

The temptation had been too much for him.

'Sch-lurpp! Sch-lurpp! Guzz-Guzz!'

Slimer was having the time of his after-life.

'Glug-glug-glug!'

He heard the familiar wail of the Ghostbuster siren. They were returning in Ecto-I. Slimer began to get worried. What would Peter say when he discovered that his melon was half-eaten?

He would not get the chance to say anything.

Slimer would make sure it was *completely* eaten.

'Sch-lurpp! Sch-lurpp! Guzz-Guzz!'
It went down beautifully.

The first thing the Ghostbusters did when they got back was to go down to the basement so that they could put their latest haul into the ecto-containment unit. Once the ghosts from the warehouse were safely locked away, the four men could carry on making fun of Janine. They followed her up to the reception area.

'Hi there, Florence Nightingale,' teased Peter.

'Yeah,' said Ray. 'You're the Lady with the Lamp.'

'Maybe you'd like a better one,' suggested Winston, grinning.

'New lamps for old!' called Egon.

They were having a lot of fun at her expense and it was annoying her. She carried the weird-looking lamp to her desk and plopped it down on the top.

'OK, low-brows,' she retaliated. 'I'll prove you're wrong about this lamp.'

'Go on, then,' urged Peter, sniggering.

'Show us, Janine,' encouraged Ray with a smirk.

They covered their mouths to stifle their amusement.

'You think it's all a joke, don't you?' she said.

'It *is*!' said Egon, chuckling.

'Just watch!' She cupped her hands together to form a loud-hailer then she opened her lungs. 'SLIII-MERRRR!'

'Where *are* you!' she bellowed.

Slimer flew into a panic. He shoved the last slice of melon into his mouth sideways. It stretched his cheeks

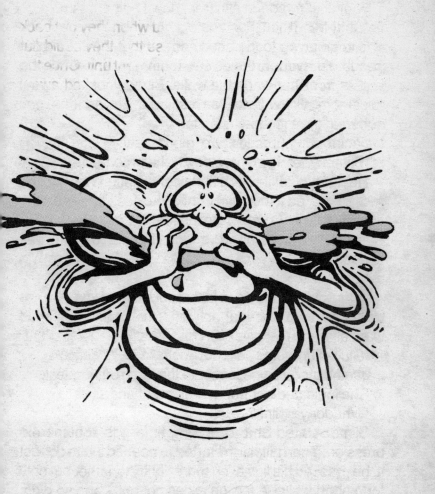

to four times their normal width. He strained to chew the giant mass but it was like trying to chew a ton of gum.

Janine summoned him from down below again.

'SLIII-MERRR!'

Slimer gave a loud hiccup and a volley of water-melon seeds sprayed around the room like machine-gun bullets, ricocheting off the walls. Slimer looked and felt miserable. His cheeks were still swollen as if he was suffering from toothache.

Janine's cry pursued him relentlessly.

'Slimer! Get down here *now*!' she ordered.

He dashed off through the air and zipped down to the reception area to hover in front of the desk. His lips were tightly sealed to keep in the last slice of melon.

The Ghostbusters were grinning but Janine was serious.

'Slimer . . .'

'Glug-glug-glug,' he said through pursed lips.

'I'm going to ask your opinion,' she continued, 'and I want an honest answer. OK?'

'Glug-glug-glug.'

Janine stood aside to reveal the lamp on her desk.

She indicated her trophy with great pride.

'Whaddaya think?'

Slimer stared at it for a long time with a blank expression. Then his mirth started to rise. Trying to control it, he pressed his lips even more tightly together but only for a short while. A few chuckles got out – and so did a few seeds.

The dark bullets shot out everywhere and bounced off

the walls. Thinking they were under attack, the Ghost-busters dived to the floor in unison.

'Aghhhh!' roared Ray as a seed hit his face.

'Somebody's shooting at us!' exclaimed Peter.

'This really gives me the pip!' yelled Egon.

'I won't take this lying down,' said Winston, lying down.

The melon seeds stopped flying and they looked up.

But there was worse to come.

The sight of the funny old lamp was too much for Slimer. He could not hold back his mirth any longer. Opening his mouth wide, he burst into a peal of laughter.

'Gluggy-gluggy-gluggy-gluggy-gluggy!'

The melon seeds came out in a rapid fire this time, shaving the heads of the Ghostbusters and forcing them to lie flat on the floor again. Slimer laughed and the barrage kept on. The whole room was a swirling mass of melon seeds.

Eventually, the attack ceased. Peter Venkman picked up one of the seeds from the floor and examined it. His anger surged.

'Hey! These are water-melon seeds.'

'Glug-glug-glug.'

'*My* water-melon seeds.'

'Glug.'

'Slimer!'

The ghost floated around uneasily in mid-air. He began to sweat profusely as Peter got up and advanced towards him. The other Ghostbusters also dragged themselves up from the floor.

'Come here, Slimer!' said Peter vengefully.

'Sch-lurpp,' whimpered the ghost.

'I *warned* you.'

Peter stepped forward to grab Slimer but in vain.

'BUUUURP!'

With a monstrous hiccup, Slimer inadvertently fired off the last of the seeds. The Ghostbusters had to dive for cover yet again.

'I'll get you for this, Slimer!' howled Peter.

'Glug-glug-glug.'

Slimer did not stop to see what his fate would be. He zipped up through the circular hole in the ceiling where the firemen's pole came down.

Peter Venkman tried to climb the pole after him.

'Come back here, you water-melon thief!'

'That ghost needs busting,' said Ray.

'Yes,' agreed Egon, brushing seeds from his overalls. 'With a melon in his mouth, he's armed and dangerous.'

'Let's go get him!' urged Winston.

Peter slid back down the pole and led the charge upstairs.

'SLIMER!!!!'

The others were close on his heels.

Janine was left alone by her desk. She watched the Ghostbusters race out then she shrugged her shoulders.

'What a bunch of bozos!'

Taking out a handkerchief, she reached for her lamp. It was very lovable. She was hurt that the others had mocked her. The lamp was a real collector's piece.

'All it needs is a good clean,' she decided.

Janine began to polish it with her handkerchief. From up above came the sounds of the Ghostbusters running around after Slimer. Janine heaved a sigh.

'Listen to 'em,' she said. 'I wish *I* was boss around here. Then things'd be different.'

Her rubbing caused the lamp to tremble, then shake, then shudder. Janine had to hold on to it firmly with both hands.

'Hey, what's going on?'

The lamp seemed to have come alive. It pulsated.

'It's getting warm!' she said in alarm.

All of a sudden, the lamp took on a shimmering glow and rainbows of energy radiated from the top. Janine had seen enough. Dropping it like a hot potato, she dived behind the desk.

'Let me outa here!'

The lamp continued to hum and vibrate even more. Then there was a blinding flash of light and a cloud of multi-coloured smoke came gushing out until it filled the room. All went deathly quiet.

Janine slowly rose up from her hiding place, her eyes wide with fear and amazement. The smoke made her cough.

'Gee! What was *in* that lamp?'

She soon got her answer and she gulped.

'Oh, my Gawd!'

A small man squatted on her desk, Hindu-style.

Thin, balding and wizened, he wore a tattered robe and a filthy turban made out of old bandages that were held together by an outsize safety-pin. He looked at Janine and gave her an oily smile. His voice was low and wimpy.

'Your wish is granted,' he said.

'What wish?'

'You are now the boss of the Ghostbusters.'

'Wh-who are you?' she stuttered.

'I'm a powerful Genie,' he said weakly.

'You?'

Janine took a closer look at him. She was not impressed. He did not look at all powerful. His turban was too big for him and it fell down over his eyes. He pushed it back up again.

'Where'd you come from?' she asked.

'The lamp,' he replied.

'In *there*?'

'Yes,' he said, giving her another oily grin. 'Since you rubbed the lamp and freed me, I must grant you three wishes.'

Janine scratched her head. She drew herself up to her full height and stared down at the curious figure on her desk. Her brow furrowed as she tried to work out what was happening. She was no longer afraid. The little man would not frighten a cat.

Eventually, she decided that the Ghostbusters were behind it all. She put her hands on her hips.

'Big joke!' she sneered.

'I'm no joke, lady,' he promised.

'Ha! Ha!'

'Don't laugh.'

'The guys put you up to this, didn't they?' she ac-
cused.

'What guys?'

'You can't fool me. I wasn't born yesterday, ya know!'

Janine stomped off and went upstairs to find them.

She was quite wrong about the Genie.

He was no joke.

As soon as she had gone, an evil look came over his
face. Crouching down, he summoned up all his energy
and his body swelled right up until his head was
touching the ceiling. Janine had left behind a small man
in funny clothes. He was now a hideous giant with ugly
teeth that were bared in a grin.

He let out a malevolent cackle.

'Ya-haahaahaahaaa!'

Grabbing the lamp he held it to his lips.

'Brothers and sisters!' he said in a hoarse whisper.
'The gateway is open and vacation begins.'

He put the lamp back on to the desk.

The real horror then started.

4

A Major Problem

The lamp began to wiggle gently, then it quivered. It was soon shaking so violently that the whole desk was bouncing about. Waves of spectral energy poured out of it and it was bathed in vivid light. There was a loud hiss as a bubble formed at the spout of the lamp. It burst immediately.

'Pop!'

A skinny spirit was left standing on the desk top. Its one eye rolled in its weird head and it checked that the coast was clear. Then it gave a whistle of delight.

'Pop!'

Another ghost came out of the lamp, a short, fat, round spirit with a wild gleam in its staring eyes. It stretched its limbs after its long imprisonment.

'Pop!'

The third spirit was the most ghoulish yet, a frightening monster who mashed his jagged teeth together in

pleasure. He looked around and emitted a ghastly scream of joy.

'Pop! Pop! Pop!'

More ghosts and ghouls came leaping from the spout.

'Pop! Pop! Pop!'

They joined together and flew around the room in a playful mood, cackling and crowing, savouring their new freedom. As they zoomed on, there were some splattering noises.

'Splurge! Splot! Splat!'

Large blobs of ectoplasm stuck to the walls.

The Ghostbusters' headquarters was haunted.

'Have fun!' urged the Genie. 'Let your hair down.'

'Wheeeeeeee!'

The Genie flew across to the window and pointed to the city outside, vulnerable and unsuspecting. It was in for a shock.

'Boys and girls – come out to play!'

After another circuit of the room, the ghosts and ghouls went out through a solid wall in a blur of colour, leaving even more blobs of ectoplasm dripping down.

'Woooooooooooooooo!'

'Enjoy yourselves!', called the Genie after them.

His wicked laugh echoed, then he vanished into thin air.

The lamp was still on the desk. It looked so harmless and innocent standing there. Janine had no idea of the damage she had done. In bringing the lamp back with her, she thought she simply had a pretty, decorative object.

But she had much more.

She had inflicted mayhem on the city of New York.

Slimer eluded them for a long time but he could not keep it up. He knew that he would have to face his punishment sooner or later, so he flew down to the floor.

The four Ghostbusters stood around him. They were not amused. Though they were all very fond of Slimer, he had to be taught how to behave properly.

Bringing up a ghost was not easy.

'You've been very naughty, Slimer,' said Egon.

'Glug-glug.'

'Don't eat what's not yours to eat,' ordered Ray.

'Especially when it's mine,' added Peter.

'Sorry, Slimer,' said Winston, 'but you got it coming.'

'Glurg!'

The ghost shook with trepidation and his eyes blinked.

Peter sat on an upright chair and Winston helped him on with a thick apron. It was to protect his lap from bits of slime.

'Glurg!'

Slimer was well-named.

He stood before Peter and he turned white with fear.

'Alright, Slimer, you little melon-muncher,' said Peter. 'You brought this on yourself.'

'Glurg!'

'Lap!'

Peter indicated his lap and Slimer reluctantly bent over it to be spanked. Peter held his right hand high.

'Glove!' he said.

'Right here,' said Egon.

He slipped a large, padded baseball glove on to Peter's hand. It was a formidable weapon and it could hurt. Slimer looked over his shoulder then closed his eyes and braced himself.

Peter Venkman was ready to administer punishment.

'Here it comes!' he warned.

But it did not.

BRING-BRING! BRING-BRING!

The alarm bell sounded and the Ghostbusters responded at once. They darted to the pole and slid down it as fast as they could. A call to action took precedence over everything.

BRING-BRING! BRING-BRING! BRING-BRING!

Slimer was dropped and fell to the floor with a thud.

'Glurg!'

He saw that they had gone and he grinned.

'Glug-glug-glug!'

Slimer had been saved by the bell.

Janine Melnitz was behind her desk when the Ghostbusters skidded to a halt in front of her. She was still angry over what she thought was a practical joke played on her. In her hand was a piece of paper with the details of the latest call.

'OK, jokesters,' she said. 'Laugh this one off.'

'What is it?' asked Ray.

'See for yourself.' She handed him the memo. 'Paranormal disturbance at the airport.'

'The airport?' repeated Egon in surprise.

'Yeah.'

'That's odd. Ghosts are usually found in old buildings with a weird history.' Egon was puzzled. 'We don't usually get calls from somewhere as modern as an airport.'

'Maybe these ghosts have just flown in on Concorde!' she quipped. 'Now – move it!'

'Whatever you say, boss,' replied Ray.

'Right behind you, boss lady,' agreed Winston.

'All the way, boss,' said Egon.

'Just tell us what to do, boss,' added Peter.

Janine gaped at the four Ghostbusters.

'*What* did you guys call me?'

'We called you boss, boss,' said Peter.

'Yeah, boss,' said Egon.

'That's right, boss,' agreed Winston.

'We always call our boss "boss", boss,' explained Ray.

There was a long pause. Peter leaned in towards her.

'You *are* the boss, aren't you?'

Janine was at a complete loss for words.

'I . . . uh . . . well . . . ah . . .'

Suddenly, the Genie popped back into view, hovering behind their heads so that she could see him while they could not. The Genie was no hideous giant now. He was the little man with the filthy turban and the wizened face.

He gave Janine a thumbs-up sign. She understood at once. He had granted her wish to be in charge. She was determined to make the most of it.

She banged the desk and gave a huge smile.

'Yes! Yes! Sure, I'm the boss!'

'Yes, boss.'

'We know that, boss.'

'So what do we do, boss?'

'Boss us!'

'OK, Ghostbusters!' she snapped. Move 'em out!'

'You got it, boss!' said Peter.

Egon, Winston, Ray and Peter went charging off to the garage. Slimer did not want to be left out either and he shot off after them. Janine positively glowed. She was their boss and they did exactly what she told them. It was a wonderful feeling.

'Pop!'

The Genie materialized in front of her again.

'Well?' he asked. 'How do you like it so far?'

'It's outrageous!' she screamed in delight.

'We aim to please.'

'I already know exactly what I want for my second wish.'

'Name it.'

Janine's eyes clouded over with a romantic haze. She clasped her hands beneath her chin and gazed rapturously skyward.

'I wish . . .'

'Yeah?'

'I wish . . . I wish . . .'

'Come on, lady. Spit it out!'

'I wish that Egon was just crazy about me.'

The Genie raised a hand and snapped his fingers.

'Done!' he promised.

Janine felt a warm sensation all over.

She hurried out to the garage where the Ghostbusters were lined up in a row beside their vehicle. Egon was holding open the front door of Ecto-I.

'What are you waiting for, guys?' she asked.

'You, boss,' they said in unison.

'Good. I'll ride in the back.'

'But you're the boss, boss,' reminded Peter. 'You can drive if you like. You make all the decisions.'

'Yeah,' she said. 'I do, don't I? OK – I drive.'

Egon helped her into the driving seat then shut the door behind her. As she looked up into his face, she saw a heart-shaped glow in his eyes. He had fallen for her at last.

'You look beautiful when you drive,' he cooed.

'Thanks, Egon.'

Peter, Winston and Ray piled into the back seat. Egon jumped in beside Janine. Slimer was strapped into a baby seat that was fixed between the two front seats. It had a miniature steering-wheel so that he could pretend to drive the car.

'Everybody, ready?' asked Janine.

'Yes, boss!'

'Let's go then!'

She stared at the array of switches and dials in front of her. It was totally confusing. Egon came to her aid and pointed to the ignition key.

'Turn this,' he explained, 'then flick that switch, pull that knob and press those buttons.'

'Check!'

She did as she was told and the engine roared into life.

Before she knew what was happening, Janine felt Ecto-I take off as if leaving the starting grid at a Grand Prix meeting. It went out through the open doors of the fire station and swung on to the main street. Janine clung to the steering-wheel and bravely fought for control.

Egon watched it all with admiration.

'That's it,' he said. 'Show it who's boss!'

Back in the reception area, the Genie peered through the window to make sure that they had gone, then he crossed to the lamp. He cupped his hands and called through them.

'Alright, everybody! Out you come!'

The lamp started to shake and wobble and hiss, then the bubbles came out of the spout thick and fast.

'Pop! Pop! Pop! Pop!'

'Party time!' said the Genie. 'Come and join us!'

'Pop! Pop! Pop! Pop!'

As the bubbles burst, dozens of ghosts, ghouls and monsters appeared on the desk, dancing around happily to celebrate their release. Their wild laughter reverberated around the room.

Ghostbuster headquarters had met a fate worse than death.

It had been taken over by ghosts!

5

Making Ghost Tracks

With its siren blaring and its light-bar flashing madly, the vehicle hared along through the streets. It was a long way out to the airport. When the Ghostbusters were on a mission, they had to move fast. Ecto-I fairly tore along.

Slimer was making appropriate noises.

'Brrrrrrrrrrm! Screeeeeeeech!'

He used his steering-wheel to drive them out of an imaginary skid, then he accelerated away. In his mind, he was the chauffeur.

'Zoooooooooom!'

Egon Spengler sat beside Janine and stared at her with a devotion that he normally kept for his spores, mould and fungus. His face was dead-pan and his voice was flat.

'You're beautiful when you're boss, Janine.'

'Am I?'

'Yeah.'

'Why . . . thank you, Egon.'

Flattered by the compliment, she turned to smile at him. She forgot that she was driving and took her eyes off the road ahead. Peter, Winston, Ray and Slimer did not. They shouted warnings.

'Look out!'

'Janine!'

'There's a truck ahead!'

'Do something!'

'Glurg!'

Janine and Egon continued to gaze into each other's eyes, oblivious to the danger that loomed up. A deafening blast from a diesel air-horn brought them out of their reverie.

'BEEEEEEEP!!!!'

Janine looked through the windscreen and froze with horror. An enormous truck was bearing down on them and a head-on collision seemed unavoidable. Ecto-1 had no chance against the bigger vehicle. It would be crushed flat.

'Yiiiiii!' exclaimed Janine.

She pulled wildly on the steering-wheel and the car missed the truck by just a few centimetres. It then zigzagged its way crazily on through the traffic before steadying itself on the right side of the street.

Peter, Ray and Winston were cowering in the back seat. Slimer had his hands over his eyes. Janine was shivering all over from the close shave.

'I was scared outa my skin,' she admitted.

Egon was quite unruffled by the lucky near-miss. His

gaze never left Janine. The heart-shaped glow was in his eyes.

'You're beautiful when you're scared outa your skin.'

'Thank you, Egon.'

Janine beamed happily at the comment.

Peter, Winston and Ray traded a worried glance in the back seat. It was Slimer who summed up their feelings.

'Yuk!'

What had *happened* to Egon?

Was the guy actually in love with her?

Kennedy Airport was a seething mass of frightened people. A big crowd was huddled outside the slime-coated main entrance. Police kept them under control. Something very strange was going on inside the building and it required the services of experts.

They soon arrived to take over.

'Zarum-zarum-zarum-zarum-zarum!'

The wailing siren stopped as Ecto-I came to a juddering halt outside the airport. Leaping out at speed, the Ghostbusters lined up with Slimer. Janine confronted them.

'Whaddaya waiting for, guys?'

'Orders,' said Peter.

'You're the boss,' reminded Winston.

'Tell us what to do, boss,' said Ray.

'Right,' decided Janine, taking charge. 'Let's go!'

She led them, at a sprint, in through the main entrance.

There were more crowds inside and they were held

back by uniformed security guards. The smell of fear was unmistakable. These people had obviously seen ghosts.

'Where are they?' shouted Janine.

'Thataway!' called a security guard, pointing.

She followed the direction of his finger and they soon came to the danger area. It was the locker area at the terminal. A bank of small, square-doored rental lockers covered one whole wall from floor to ceiling. When the Ghostbusters came sliding up, everything seemed to be quiet.

'Looks like we missed the party,' noted Peter.

'You never know with ghosts,' said Winston.

'Can you get a residual reading, Egon?' asked Ray, studying the lockers. There was no answer. 'Egon!' he repeated.

But Egon was busy elsewhere. In love.

With a simpering smile on his face, he was gazing adoringly at Janine as if nothing else in the world mattered to him. His PKE meter dangled from his hand, clicking and blinking away without him even noticing. Egon was entranced.

'EGON!' yelled Ray.

'What? What?'

Egon came out of his trance and snapped into action. He directed his meter at the lockers to see if it could detect any Psycho-Kinetic Energy left behind or generated by ghosts.

There was another PKE meter at work as well.

Slimer.

'Snuff-snuff-snuff!'

Floating along the lockers, he sniffed them in turn.

'Snuff-snuff-snuff-snuff!'

Slimer stopped in front of a locker that was right in the middle of the bank. He pointed to it excitedly. They waited and watched. Ecto-slime started to ooze out of the locker.

'Snuff-snuff!' said Slimer triumphantly.

'Bull's-eye!' announced Winston.

'Good work, Slimer,' said Ray.

'It takes one to know one,' noted Winston.

Peter stepped forward and spoke politely to Janine.

'May I handle this one, boss?'

'Go for it, big guy,' she said.

Peter tapped on the metal door of the locker.

'Knock, knock!' he sang.

'Who's there?' asked a gruff voice from inside.

'Dishes.'

The locker door opened and a gruesome ghost peered out.

'Dishes who?'

'Dishes the Ghostbusters!' yelled Peter. 'Come on out!'

Every single locker opened to reveal a ghost inside.

'Ghostbusters!' they cried. 'Aghhhhhhhh!'

Zipping back into their lockers, they slammed their doors simultaneously. The Ghostbusters had them cornered. Janine was enjoying the experience of giving the orders.

'OK, guys,' she said with authority. 'Activate your Proton Packs. We'll flush 'em out.'

Egon gave her another simpering smile of adoration.

'You're beautiful when you flush 'em out.'

The Ghostbusters flicked the switches on their packs and the units surged up to full power with the familiar hum. Janine waved them into a line and they aimed their guns at the wall lockers, bracing their feet against the vibrations that would come. Slimer hid behind Ray's shoulder and peered out cautiously.

'Ready?' asked Janine.

'Ready, boss,' they replied.

'OK, then. Aim and . . .'

Janine got no further. Before she could give the order to fire, the locker doors were flung open and a tidal wave of ghosts swept out and slimed them all over.

'Wheeeeeeeeeeee!'

'Hoooooooooooooo!'

'Yaaaaaaaaaaaaaah!'

Howling and cackling, the army of ghosts flew off through the air, going down a corridor and vanishing around a corner.

The Ghostbusters were left beaten, bewildered and sprawled on the ground. Janine blew a lock of hair away from her eyes. She could not understand why the ghosts were so excited.

'What are *they* so happy about?'

'Good question,' said Egon. 'Their behaviour doesn't fit the normal patterns.'

'I know what makes them happy,' suggested Peter, grinning.

'What?' asked Janine.

'High spirits!'

The others groaned.

The ghosts, meanwhile, had made their way to the baggage area at the terminal. Locked luggage was trundling along on the conveyor belt. The ghosts knew what to do. Whooshing down from the air, they disappeared into various items of luggage, sliming the outsides as they did so. The conveyor belt took them through a hatch and towards a waiting truck.

Guns at the ready, the Ghostbusters burst in.

'Now where'd they go?' asked Winston.

'Search me,' said Peter.

'Egon,' called Ray.

But Egon was once again preoccupied. Though he was holding out his PKE meter, he was looking at Janine with puppy dog eyes. Embarrassed by it, she grabbed his limp arm and lifted it up so that she could look at the meter herself.

'Uh, we've got a reading, but it's fading fast.'

'So is Egon!' noted Peter with irritation.

'This way!' urged Janine.

She led the team at a run through a door and out on to the tarmac. A jet aircraft stood nearby with a mobile staircase running up to its door. The Ghostbusters looked everywhere but there was no sign of a ghost.

They did not see the cases tumbling into the back of a

59

truck behind them. Concealed inside the luggage was a deadly cargo. The truck drew away and crossed over to the hold of the aircraft. At the flick of a switch, the luggage was automatically loaded into the plane.

'Tell us what to do, boss,' asked Ray.

'Yeah,' said Winston. 'Make a decision.'

'OK,' said Janine. 'Let's start checking the planes. Maybe we'll get lucky.'

She raced up the steps of the nearby aircraft and the others followed her with Slimer bringing up the rear. Down in the cargo hold, muffled sniggers were breaking out.

The Ghostbusters were aboard the plane.

But so were the ghosts.

It would be a horrendous flight!

6

High Jinks

The Jumbo jet stood calmly on the tarmac. Every seat was taken and all the passengers were aboard. They had no idea what lay ahead. They were expecting a routine flight to Miami where they were due to spend their vacation. Relaxed and comfortable, they chatted happily to each other.

Terror lurked in store for them.

Mirth and mischief increased down in the cargo hold as the ghosts popped out of their suitcases one by one. There were male and female spirits there as well as weird animals of every description. Inside their cases, they had all found something to put on and they now emerged with flowered shirts, fishing hats, sun glasses, summer dresses and much more. Many of them had cameras around their necks.

They were going on vacation as well.

'Yee-ha-ha!'

'Hip-hip-hip-hip!'

'Goooooooooo!'

'Ziz-ziz-ziz-ziz.'

Four of them got together and whizzed up a ventilation shaft. It brought them out in the empty cockpit and they looked around with sniggering satisfaction.

There could not be a better start to their pranks.

Janine and the Ghostbusters walked up and down the aisles on their search. They peered under the seats and into the overhead storage compartments. The passengers stared at them with growing unease. Winston tried to reassure them with a friendly grin.

'Relax, folks, we're just browsing.'

'Yeah,' said Ray. 'Anybody seen a ghost?'

The passengers flew into a panic.

'GHOSTS!'

They dived under their seats in fear. Winston clicked his tongue and turned to Ray Stantz.

'Silver tongue strikes again!'

Suddenly, jet engines burst into life and the whole aircraft began to throb. Janine and the Ghostbusters were puzzled.

'This plane is not due to leave yet,' said Peter.

'It *can't* leave,' argued Janine. 'There's no pilot.'

'So why are the engines on?' wondered Ray.

'Maybe the mechanic is testing them,' said Janine.

'Oh, good,' added Ray with evident relief. 'I thought for one terrible moment that there might be ghosts in the cockpit.'

'Wheeeeeeeeeee!'

Ray Stantz had guessed right.

Four hideous ghosts appeared in the doorway to the cockpit. They looked around the passengers with malicious glee. They were having real fun.

'Fasten your safety belts!' they sang together.

Then they dived into the cockpit and slammed the door.

Panic increased among the passengers and screams rang out.

'Ohhhhhhhhh!'

'Get me oooooooooooff!'

'Stop this plaaaaaaaaane!'

'I'm afraid of ghooooooooosts!'

Peter Venkman rushed across to Janine.

'Calm them down somehow!' he suggested.

'Yeah,' said Winston. 'You're the boss!'

'Do something!' urged Ray.

'You're beautiful when you do something,' said Egon.

Janine did her best to shout above the tumult.

'Listen to me, everybody!' she screeched. 'You are not in any real danger. There is no way that this plane could take off without a pilot.'

'Vrrrrrrrrrm!'

She was sent somersaulting down the aisles as the aircraft taxied off towards the runway. The door slammed shut and the seat-belt signs lighted up over the passengers' heads. With gathering speed, the plane surged on. It obviously did not need a pilot.

It had four ghosts at the controls instead.

Screams and shouts got louder as the plane reached

the take-off runway. It paused to let its engines build up power, then it rocketed off down the tarmac. With everyone hanging on for dear life, it reached top speed then lifted its nose to the skies.

As it soared up into the sky, Janine and the Ghostbusters were hurtled down the aisle again. They collapsed together in a pile. Egon was the first up and he lifted Janine up with care.

'Thanks, Egon.'

'Any time.'

Slimer jumped into one of the seats belonging to the flight crew and strapped himself in. The Ghostbusters clung for safety to whatever came to hand. As the plane continued its steep ascent, everyone was more or less lying backwards. It was eerie.

In the cockpit, the ghosts were having a ball.

'Yeeeee-haaaah!'

'Whooo-heeeeh!'

They pulled back the control yokes as hard as they could so that the plane was climbing almost vertically. It was like being on a switch-back at a fairground and they were loving every minute of it.

'Hiiii-deeee-hiiii!'

Back in the passenger compartment, everyone was still wide-eyed with terror and shaking like leaves. The Ghostbusters did their best to introduce a note of calm.

'Easy, folks,' said Winston. 'Everything's gonna be fine.'

'Yes,' said Peter. 'No harm will come to you.'

'There's no chance of that,' promised Ray.

'No,' announced Janine. '*We're* here to protect you.'

'I'm glad of that,' said Egon, smiling at her.

The plane levelled off slightly and a door opened at the end of the aisle. Two uniformed stewardesses backed out with food trolleys. The meals were steaming hot and just what was needed to distract the passengers.

'See?' called Janine. 'Here comes lunch!'

'They're taking care of us,' noted Winston.

'Yes,' said Peter. 'This is Ghost Airlines at your service.'

He spoke too soon.

The two stewardesses turned around to face the passengers. They were ghosts in disguise. Pulling off their wigs, they bared their fangs and leered at everyone.

'Surprise! Surprise!'

'Noooooooooooo!' howled the passengers.

'Yeeeeeeeees!' answered the ghosts.

They hopped on to their trolleys and rode them as they slid rapidly down the aisles. Grabbing piles of food, they glared around at the hapless passengers.

'Lunch is on us!' said the first ghost.

'Make that – on *you*!' corrected the second one.

Firing at will, they began to hurl the food at the screaming passengers. Some of it scored direct hits and some of it smacked into a wall before dripping down over the people below. One man stood up to protest and got a meat pie full in the face.

Slimer was jealous.

'Glug-glug-glug!'

Food was flying everywhere but in his direction.

'Glug-glug-glug!'

People were getting plastered left, right and centre.

'Sch-lurpp! Sch-lurpp!'

Slimer finally got his share. As a huge hamburger was thrown at him, he produced a catcher's mitt, slipped it on and caught the food in mid-air. It went straight into his mouth.

'Glug-glug-glug!'

They could throw food at him all day. Slimer loved it.

Ice cream and jelly and blancmange now joined the hail storm. Everybody was covered with the mess in a matter of seconds.

'This is worse than being slimed,' ventured Peter.

'What is?' asked Ray, looking around.

A wobbly white blancmange slapped into his face.

'*That* is,' explained Peter.

'Ugh!' From under the blobs, Ray agreed.

The nightmare flight became even worse.

'Zeeeeeeeeeeeeeeeeh!'

Out of the fresh air nozzles above the heads of the passengers came an endless stream of smaller ghosts and spirits, cackling, wailing and doing all they could to spread more terror.

One big, fat, dark-haired man sat there in agony as a tiny monster first tweaked his nose then yanked off his wig and threw it aside. The monster then used his bald pate as a skating arena and he slid gracefully around on it.

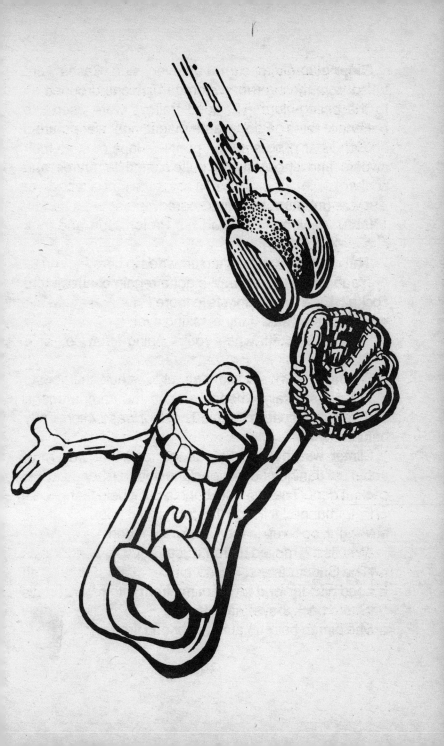

Other outrages occurred on every side. Cases were taken from the overhead storage-bins and dropped on to the passengers. The food trolleys were used like battering rams. Books and magazines were hurled about. Other ghosts sat on people's laps or stole their sweets and chocolate or pulled off their shoes and socks.

It was unbearable. Panic soared.

Peter Venkman grabbed his Proton Gun and took aim.

'No!' warned Ray. 'It's too crowded in here.'

'Yeah,' said Winston. 'We gotta regain control in the cockpit. Let's hit the ghosts in there.'

'Follow me!' said Janine, taking over.

'You're beautiful when you're being followed,' said Egon.

Seeing the Ghostbusters about to attack, the ghosts made a last scary whoosh around the compartment, then retreated to the cockpit. The door was locked firmly behind them.

Slimer was busy eating all the food that was lying about but Janine and the four Ghostbusters raced to the cockpit door. They tried its handle but it held fast.

Peter banged a fist on the connecting door.

'Alright, open up in there!' he demanded.

'Who is it?' replied a gruff voice.

'The Ghostbusters!'

Loud cackles and howls came from within.

'Stand back, boys!' said Janine.

She aimed her gun at the door and fired.

'Booooooooooom!'

A withering burst of energy blasted a big hole in the door where the handle used to be. The door swung open and the Ghostbusters went into the cockpit.

But it was completely empty!

A gust of wind blew in through an open window. They peered out through the glass and got a dreadful surprise. The ghosts were parachuting gently towards the earth. They had escaped.

The Ghostbusters were stuck in a runaway plane.

With no pilot.

They did not have a ghost of a chance.

7

Spooky Landing

The aircraft was still travelling at high speed but it was losing height rapidly. Without anyone at the controls, it had gone into a dive and was slicing its way through thick, white clouds. All around it were cackling ghosts who were parachuting to safety.

Ray Stantz closed the window and turned to Janine.

'*Now* whadda we do?' he asked.

'Why look at me?' she said.

'Because you're the boss.'

'Yeah, you're the boss,' agreed Winston.

'You're beautiful when you're the boss,' said Egon.

'That's right,' added Peter. 'You're the boss, Janine.' He frowned and rubbed his chin. 'Though I'm not exactly sure why.'

'Nor am I,' said Janine to herself.

Being the boss wasn't quite so much fun any more.

Winston looked through the windscreen and called out.

'Hey, we're about to land!'

'Thank goodness!' said Janine with relief.

'Great!' said Peter.

'Best news so far,' argued Ray.

'What goes up must come down,' reminded Egon seriously.

'Just one problem,' Winston pointed out.'

'Is there?' asked Janine.

'Yeah – we're just about to land on Fifth Avenue.'

The other Ghostbusters were horrified.

'Aghhhhhh!' screamed Janine.

'Ohhhhhhh!' howled Ray.

'Eeeeeee!' shouted Peter.

'But we *can't* land on Fifth Avenue,' said Egon, treating the matter like a scientific problem. 'It has no runway.'

'It has now,' countered Winston. 'It *is* a runway.'

As they gazed through the windscreen, the concrete canyon of Fifth Avenue came shooting up towards them. It was teeming with pedestrians and the traffic jams were long and noisy. To come down there would be to cause the most appalling accident. Thousands of innocent lives would be lost.

Including those of the Ghostbusters.

And – for the second time – that of Slimer.

'Glurg!' he protested.

'Time for action, Janine!' urged Peter.

'What must I do?'

'Boss us!'

'Right,' she said to him. 'Come on!'

74

She leaped over into the pilot's seat and settled herself down. Peter followed suit and landed in the co-pilot's seat. Reaching for the yokes, they wrestled to control the aircraft as it plummeted ever nearer to the ground.

'Glurg!'

Slimer had seen enough. Eyes like saucers, he turned away and dived for cover into a pocket in Ray's overall. Slimer did not wish to end up splattered over the sidewalk in Fifth Avenue.

'Good luck!' called Winston to the two new pilots.

'We'll need it,' admitted Janine.

'Hold on to your lunch, everybody!' warned Peter.

'This should be worth seeing,' said Egon with interest. 'If we touch down here, you'll set an aeronautical precedent.'

'We'd rather live,' said Winston hopefully.

'Here we go!' called Janine.

The aircraft flew down between the skyscrapers that lined Fifth Avenue. Swerving erratically from side to side, it went along the thoroughfare to the shock and amazement of those below. Pedestrians stared, shoppers rushed out to gape, policemen were hypnotised, street vendors mesmerised, taxi drivers were transfixed and every vehicle came to a grinding halt.

They were looking up at something astonishing.

It was the end of the world.

The Ghostbusters were at the controls.

'This is awful!' exclaimed Janine.

'I'd rather be up here than down there,' argued Peter.

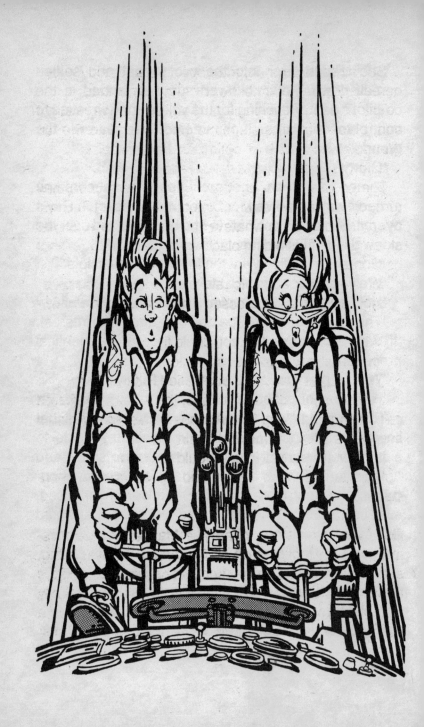

'I'd rather be far away from *both* places!' said Ray.

'Glurg!' agreed Slimer from inside his pocket.

The speed of the plane had set up a huge draught and it blew newspapers and rubbish high into the air. Winston tried to take an optimistic view of it all.

'Look at that! We get a ticker-tape reception.'

The buildings of Manhattan were just a blur as they rushed past the windows of the cockpit. Egon, Ray and Winston clung on to whatever they could reach. Slimer peeped out of his hiding place, saw the worst, then shot back again.

Janine continued to flick switches and press buttons.

Ray Stantz was impressed with her apparent know-how.

'Whoa! I didn't realise you could fly, Janine.'

'I can't!' she wailed in desperation.

'That makes two of us,' confessed Peter.

Tilting madly from side to side, the aircraft continued its horrific flight along Fifth Avenue. It missed a collision by a hair's breadth time and again.

Sooner or later, their luck would run out.

The Ghostbusters would end up as ghosts themselves.

On a roof-top garden nearby, a Manhattan business-man was enjoying an off-duty moment. He was a big, sleek, portly character in a suit and he was watering the flowers and shrubs with a can. The massive underbelly of the jet roared past only inches above his head. In a flash, the trees and shrubs were stripped of all their leaves and the garden lost all its topsoil and roofing materials.

But it was the man who suffered most.

The force of the wind-blast sent him bowling over backwards and stripped him of all his clothing down to his vest and his spotted boxer shorts. A large patch of his curly hair was torn away and his cigar was frayed.

'Say, what *is* this?' he protested.

As he gazed up, another strange sight greeted him. Dozens of ghosts and ghouls were floating down in parachutes like an invading army. Their weird cackles echoed through Manhattan.

The man ran off with a scream of absolute terror.

The aircraft, meanwhile, continued to behave exactly as it wished. Though Janine and Peter worked hard at the controls, they could not seem to lift the plane up above the skyscrapers. They made a final effort to take charge and the aircraft at last responded. Still banked, to avoid hitting any buildings, it rose up with awesome power and headed for the clouds again.

Janine and Peter had saved the day.

'Great flying!' congratulated Winston.

'How about looping the loop?' joked Ray.

'It was nothing,' said Peter modestly.

'We got lucky, that's all,' added Janine.

'You're beautiful when you're lucky,' said Egon.

The other Ghostbusters willingly agreed to that.

So did Slimer.

'Glurg!'

The plane had levelled out again now and it was flying across the roof of Manhattan. Another danger threatened. As they skimmed along the Hudson River, the daunting figure of the Statue of Liberty stood up before them.

'We're going to hit her!' warned Winston.

'Do something, boss!' urged Ray.

'Go on, Janine!' encouraged Peter.

Unable to alter the course of the plane, she put her fingers in her mouth and gave her ear-shattering whistle. Even above the roar of the engines, it was clearly heard. The Statue of Liberty took due note. When they were just about to crash into it, the Statue ducked and let them pass. It quickly resumed its posture as if nothing had happened.

The Ghostbusters blinked in blank disbelief.

Had they seen what they thought they'd seen?

It was Ray Stantz who spotted something in the distance. He pointed a finger at the windscreen to draw their attention to what he had seen.

'The airport! There's the airport!'

Slimer popped out to see for himself.

'Glug-glug-glug!' he said with pleasure.

'You've done it, Janine!' said Winston. 'Great stuff!'

Pleased with her success, she grabbed the microphone.

'Ghostbusters to tower,' she said. 'Ghostbusters to tower. We're coming in!'

Putting the microphone aside, she pushed the control yoke forward and the plane went into a nose dive. Ray,

Egon, Winston and Slimer were all spread-eagled on the floor, thrown there by the force and steepness of the descent.

Ray's voice was high-pitched and worried.

'Uh, boss . . .?'

'Yeah?' asked Janine.

'Could we come in a little slower?'

'The sooner we get down, the sooner we'll be safe.'

'That's logical,' decided Egon. 'I think.'

'Brace yourselves, everyone,' warned Peter.

'Yeah,' said Janine. 'It could be a bumpy landing.'

She flicked a switch on the control panel and the wheels unfolded beneath the plane. It was an encouraging start. So far, so good. Now for the difficult bit.

'There's the runway, Peter!' noted Janine.

'It looks so narrow,' he complained.

'We'll hit it bang in the middle.'

Her promise was all too accurate.

Coming in far too fast, and at far too sharp an angle, the aircraft touched down on the runway with a tell-tale noise.

'SCREEEEEEEEEEEECH!'

Its wheels bounced and its tyres screamed as the brakes were applied. The rubber began to smoulder, then it burst into flames so that the tyres were shredded to pieces in seconds.

'STOP, boss!' yelled Ray.

'I'm trying to!' she said.

'Why doesn't it slow *down*?' wondered Winston.

Janine and Peter kept their feet down hard on the brakes.

'CRUUUUUUUUUUUUUNCH!'

The tyres had gone now and the rims had been worn away to nothing. All that was holding the plane up were the wheel struts and they were sending up a cloud of dust as they ploughed into the tarmac. The terminal building was ahead and they were aimed straight at it. A terrible crash seemed inevitable.

Brows perspiring, the Ghostbusters hung on for all they were worth. Slimer, dangling from the ceiling, had his eyes shut and his hands closed together in prayer.

'Muff-muff-muff.'

The struts beneath the plane could not take the friction and they were being ground away to nothing. Without warning, the plane was skidding along on its belly in a shower of sparks. As it hurtled along, it was digging a trench in the runway.

The sparks turned to fire and black smoke enveloped the whole aircraft. They could see nothing through the windscreen and waited for the moment of impact when they hit the building ahead.

But the crash never came.

Still covered in a cloud of foul smelling smoke, the plane finally ground to a halt only metres away from the building. They had made it. When the smoked cleared, however, they saw that the aircraft had not. All the superstructure had been destroyed by the landing. The only thing that remained were the rows of seats in which the frightened passengers were still strapped.

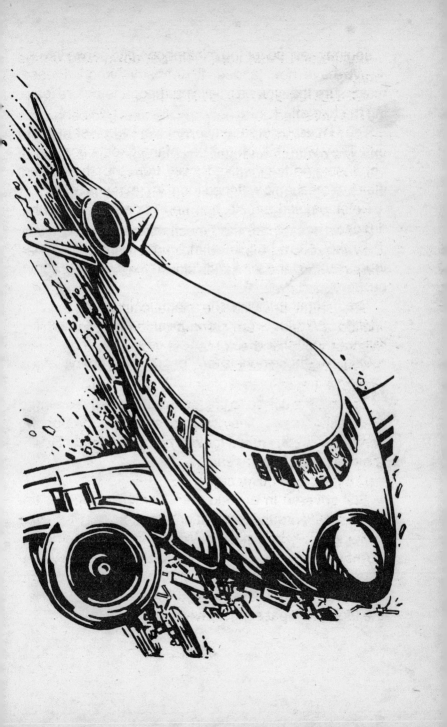

Janine reached for the microphone and spoke into it.

'We have now landed at Kennedy Airport. Please make sure that you have all your baggage before leaving the aircraft.'

The Ghostbusters themselves were the first to jump out. They were still on the trail of the ghosts and could not linger. As they walked away from the shell of the plane, a mechanic watched them in utter amazement.

Peter paused beside him and nodded back to the debris.

'Brakes aren't bad,' he said, 'and the sunroof's a nice touch, but we think we'll wait for the new models to come out.'

The mechanic dropped his spanner in shock.

They had ruined millions of dollars' worth of aircraft.

The Ghostbusters were not concerned.

Catching those ghosts took priority over everything.

8

Ghosts in the Groove

The flight had been an ordeal but the Ghostbusters quickly shrugged it off. They had work to do and could not stop to feel sorry for themselves. Charging through the airport terminal, they came out by the main entrance. Ecto-I was still parked at the kerb.

'Extra! Extra! Read all about it!'

A newsboy was selling papers nearby.

'City overrun by ghosts!'

'Hear that?' said Winston to the others.

'Hundreds of hauntings reported!' yelled the boy.

Winston handed him a dollar and took one of the newspapers. Its front page was covered in details of the hauntings. Banner headlines were used to warn of the danger of the ghosts.

'They're everywhere,' said Winston, reading the paper. 'The amusement park, the beach, the baseball stadium!'

'Gosh!' exclaimed Ray. 'All the fun spots.'

'It's almost like they're on vacation,' said Peter.

'Precisely,' agreed Egon, trying to work something out.

'Let's go get 'em!' ordered Janine.

They leaped into the vehicle with their boss at the wheel.

'Where are we going, Janine?' asked Ray.

'Central Park.'

'But why?'

'Because there's a pop concert there today.'

'I don't *like* pop concerts,' complained Ray.

'I do!' said Winston. 'I dig real groovy music.'

'We're not going there for the music,' explained Janine.

'Then what *are* we going there for?' asked Ray.

'Ghosts.'

'Ghosts?'

'Yeah,' she replied. 'You know, Ray. Those whacky weirdoes that we're supposed to bust for a living.'

'But why Central Park?'

'Because of what you just said.'

'Me?' Ray was baffled.

'All the fun spots,' Janine continued. 'You pointed out that these ghosts like a bit of excitement. My guess is they'll check into Central Park pretty soon. With a pop concert going on there, they'd hate to miss out on the fun.'

'Well done, Janine,' said Winston. 'That's brilliant!'

'You're beautiful when you're brilliant,' said Egon.

'Let's just hope I'm *right*!'

She pressed the accelerator and Ecto-I shot away.

Central Park had attracted hundreds of thousands of teenage fans for the open-air concert. The band was called the Hairy Honchos and they lived up to their name. They had hair that came halfway down their backs – and the men had long beards as well. Their music was loud and brash and it had a terrific beat. The audience loved them.

'Hurrah! More! More! More!'

The Ghostbusters arrived on the scene and parked their vehicle. They joined the crowd and got their first glimpse of the Hairy Honchos. Slimer was not among their fans.

'Glurg!'

'Know something?' said Peter.

'What?' asked Winston.

'These guys are more frightening to look at than ghosts.'

'Back off, man. They got a cool sound.'

'Only if you're stone deaf, Winston.'

'What's wrong with the Hairy Honchos?'

'See for yourself,' said Peter. 'Take that lead singer, for instance. That man is scary.'

'That man is a woman,' explained Winston.

'With a voice like that? He can't be!'

'He is a *she*, Peter.'

Winston was proved right within seconds.

The lead singer was holding the microphone and dancing to the beat of the music. Suddenly, an unseen hand whisked the microphone away and it floated through the air as if suspended on an invisible thread.

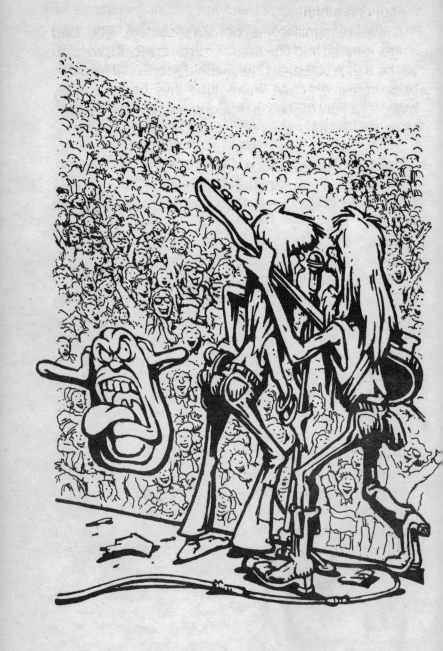

'Aghhhhhhhhh!'

It was recognisably a woman's scream. The lead singer jumped into the arms of the drummer for comfort but he had problems of his own. No sooner did he stand back from the set of drums than they began to play louder than ever. His drumsticks were nowhere near the skins and yet they were pounding out noise.

'Ghosts!' exclaimed Janine.

'Musical ghosts!' added Egon.

'I like their rhythm,' conceded Winston.

'They're better than the Hairy Honchos,' agreed Peter.

But the Hairy Honchos were no longer quite so hairy.

'Noooooooooooooo!'

A large pair of scissors floated through the air and snipped away at hair and beards. The band yelled its protest but the scissors kept working and the stage was soon covered with piles of black hair.

Thinking it was all part of the concert, the fans pushed forward to grab the hair as souvenirs. None of the musicians held their instruments any longer and yet the music went on with increased volume.

'They're not Hairy Honchos now,' said Peter with a laugh.

'More like the Bald Bozos,' noted Ray.

'It's the Groovy Ghosts we want,' reminded Janine.

'Yes, boss!' agreed Egon, saluting.

'But where are they?' said Winston.

'Why don't they come out and fight?' said Ray.

The ghosts must have heard him.

They came out to fight with a vengeance, swooping down from the trees like a flock of birds and causing havoc on all sides. At the sight of the great horde in the sky, the fans went into a terminal panic and scattered madly.

'Heeeeeeeelp!'

'Ghooooooooosties!'

'Buuuuuuuuust 'em, somebody!'

'That's us!' said Janine, hearing the cry.

Guns at the ready, the Ghostbusters surged towards the stage where the music was still being played by unseen musicians. Flying monsters wheeled above them in the sky and eluded their fire. Cackling ghouls dropped piles of cones and leaves on to them to slow them down. Central Park was in complete chaos.

'Some pop concert!' moaned Peter.

'Pop! Pop! Pop!'

More ghosts popped into sight on stage.

'Pop! Pop! Pop! Pop!'

They came out through the skins of the drums. They emerged from the guitars. They broke loose from the synthesizer. Playing a deafening melody of their own, they leaped about in a ghostly dance that was quite macabre.

It sent the fans running even faster.

The Ghostbusters closed in on the stage.

'Hit 'em from every angle!' commanded Janine.

'Yes, boss.'

'Just give the word, boss.'

'We're standing by, boss.'

'Say when, boss.'

'NOW!'

Janine's shout was seconds too late.

As the Ghostbusters fired their Proton Guns, beams of energy shot towards the stage but the ghosts had somehow vanished. All that the guns did was to destroy the expensive equipment on stage. Guitars shrivelled in the heat, the drums melted and the synthesizer fell to pieces. The giant speakers keeled over and were smashed into fragments.

Having wrecked the concert, the ghosts streaked away to spread their mischief elsewhere. The Ghostbusters were left standing in the middle of the debris. They might have escaped the threat of the ghosts now, but another threat loomed.

'Come here, you finks!'

A big, bald, brawny young man advanced on them.

'Who are you?' asked Janine politely.

'A Hairy Honcho!' he growled. 'And that was my equipment you just destroyed.'

'It was an accident,' explained Janine.

'So is this!' replied the man.

Picking up the scissors, he clicked them menacingly and charged at them. None of the Ghostbusters felt in need of a haircut and they would not have chosen him as their barber in any case. They beat a hasty retreat and jumped into their car. They were glad when it pulled away.

The Hairy Honcho waved his weapon at them.

'Fab concert!' called Peter from the car.

The Honcho pulled out what was left of his hair.

'Yeah,' added Peter. 'Real spooky music, man.'

Central Park would never be quite the same again.

Inside the car, they tried to fathom it all out. It seemed as if the ghosts were on some kind of holiday together. They were on a spending spree of mayhem and madness. It was disturbing.

'Where are they all coming from?' asked Janine.

'I have a theory,' said Egon. 'Somewhere – somehow – an inter-dimensional gate has been opened between the spirit world and our own. Unless we find it and seal it, the flow of energy will become too powerful to stop.'

Janine gulped. She saw that she might be to blame.

Ray Stantz turned to her for guidance.

'Whaddya think, boss?'

'I think I'm gonna be sick.'

'You're beautiful when you're sick,' said Egon.

His routine admiration got on her nerves this time.

'Listen,' she snapped. 'Will you knock it off, Egon!'

He stared at her, hurt and jolted by her outburst.

'Sure,' he murmured.

'Now, come on!' she insisted. 'We've got work to do.'

They had to rescue the city of New York.

9

Back in the Trap

The sky over Manhattan was golden now, as the light of day faded. Somewhere in the distance, a column of ethereal energy went straight up into the air for several hundred metres, then splayed out in four sinuous branches that spread to the four corners of the city. It was very dramatic and alarmingly supernatural.

Ecto-I cruised through the streets with Janine driving. Egon was beside her and Slimer occupied the baby seat between them. Peter, Ray and Winston lounged in the rear of the car.

All six of them sat forward when they saw the extra-ordinary sight through the windscreen. It was quite dazzling.

'Holy smoke!' said Winston.

'Not smoke,' corrected Egon. 'Spectral energy.'

'We've got 'em!' announced Peter.

'That's where the ghosts are,' agreed Janine.

'Glug-glug-glug.'

Slimer did not want to be left out of the discussion.

'Wow!' exclaimed Ray. 'I've never seen such a massive concentration of spectral energy.'

'Yeah,' said Winston with sympathy. 'I pity the poor dudes who live in *that* neighbourhood.'

The car headed towards the brilliant glow at top speed.

The building to which they were racing was now pulsing with energy. It was acting like a powerful magnet on its surroundings. Trash and loose objects were sucked from the neighbourhood to form huge piles outside the front door. Spirits and demons whizzed around every room and made it blaze with unnatural light. Some of them got into the chimneys and the ventilation system, fighting their way upwards until they came out on the roof. The column of spectral energy now stretched even higher into the sky, like a giant staircase to heaven.

Except that these ghosts came from the other address.

Ecto-I skidded to a halt outside the building.

The Ghostbusters took one look at it and gulped.

'Oh no!' said Peter.

'Those poor dudes are *us*!' groaned Winston.

It was the old fire station. Ghostbuster headquarters.

They had been dispossessed by evil spirits.

Egon Spengler took out a strange pair of binoculars that were hand-built, high-tech, electronically enhanced and unique. He trained them on the building.

Everyone feared that the captured ghosts had got loose.

'Is it the containment system?' asked Ray with concern.

'No,' said Egon.

'Then what?'

'Give me time.'

The binoculars scanned the interior of the fire station with their X-ray vision. The brick walls were only a hazy, transparent presence. Egon had designed the binoculars himself. The optics contained cross-hairs and peripheral digital displays that reflected the degree of magnifying power being used.

'See anything odd?' asked Peter.

'Not yet,' said Egon. 'It all looks very normal.'

His binoculars then locked in on an object in the reception area. It was standing on the desk and giving off a rainbow of energy. Spirits of all shapes and sizes were streaming out of it with great glee.

'It's that old brass lamp of Janine's,' decided Egon.

'My lamp?' Janine was covered in guilt. 'Ohhhhh . . .'

The Ghostbusters all turned to look at her.

'What's up?' asked Winston.

'You've gone white,' noted Ray.

'Anything you want to tell us?' invited Peter.

'Let's have it,' said Egon quietly.

Janine gazed woefully at the house then back at them.

'It was my fault,' she confessed.

'How?' pressed Egon.

'When I released the Genie from the lamp, I must've released all these ghosts, too.'

The others – including Slimer – spoke in a chorus.

'The *Genie*?'

'Don't worry,' reassured Janine. 'I'll fix this in a jiffy.'

The others exchanged another look of bewilderment.

'A jiffy?' they asked.

Janine snapped her fingers and the scrawny little Genie appeared in the car in a flash, hovering in the air before her.

'You called?' he said.

'Glurg!!!'

A pale-faced Slimer sought refuge in Ray's pocket again.

The Ghostbusters dropped their jaws at the sight of the peculiar little man with the turban. Was he really a *Genie*?

'Yes!' replied Janine. 'I called you.'

'Whaddya want?' asked the Genie in a bored voice.

'For my third and final wish, I want all these ghosts to return to the lamp *immediately*!'

The Genie folded his arms and grinned broadly.

'Forget it, lady.'

'But I've got three wishes.'

'Have you?'

'Yes! You promised.'

'I lied,' he admitted with his oily grin. 'I had to keep you busy while my fellow spirits escaped from our own dreary dimension into . . .' He gave an expansive gesture. 'Fun City!'

'Poof!'

The Genie had disappeared into thin air again.

Janine and the Ghostbusters were stunned by it all.

Peter shrugged his shoulders sadly.

'Looks like we're up a creek without a Genie.'

But Ray Stantz had more optimism. With a screwdriver in one hand and a pair of pliers in the other, he worked away at some cables in his lap. Slimer put out his head to watch.

'Maybe we're not,' argued Ray, holding up a wreath of electrical wires. 'By combining the power of these portable ecto-traps, we may be able to reverse the polarity of the lamp and turn it into one big trap that sucks all the ghosts back into their own world.'

'Fantastic, Ray!' shouted Winston.

'Terrific!' agreed Peter.

'Scientifically stupendous!' congratulated Egon.

'There's only one hitch,' explained Ray, holding up two electrical wires with suction cup connectors on them. 'Who's going inside the station to connect it up?'

The Ghostbusters were all reluctant to volunteer.

'The risk factor is dangerously high,' noted Egon.

'Don't look at me,' complained Peter. 'I already took out the trash.'

'And I've got this bad . . . cough!' said Winston, coughing badly.

'That leaves me,' said Ray, 'and I won't take the chance.'

Slimer leaped out of his pocket and jumped up and down with such urgency that he slimed them all. They yelled at him but he pointed through the windscreen.

Someone had gathered up the two electrical cables. Holding them in one hand, she was hanging on to a street lamp with the other so that the raging wind did not drag her to the front door.

It was Janine.

'Come back!' yelled Winston.

'It's too dangerous!' warned Egon.

'Get away!' advised Ray.

'No way!' she shouted. 'I caused this mess and I've gotta straighten it out!'

The street lamp was suddenly uprooted and she was drawn feet-first into the house by the screaming wind. Watching from the comparative safety of Ecto-I, the Ghostbusters were mortified.

Egon had a special reason to fear for her.

'Ja-niiiiiiine!' he howled.

She, meanwhile, had been blown inside and finished up flat on her face in front of her desk. The brass lamp glowed away, blindingly incandescent as the plasmatic stream of ghosts and spirits spewed upwards from it like a supernatural Roman candle.

Squinting in the glare, Janine held the suction cups and moved them slowly towards the lamp. Just as she was about to lock them into position, the Genie appeared on the desk.

'Stop!' he ordered. 'Don't touch that! Don't! Don't!'

'Oh yeah?' she retorted. 'Outa the way, creep!'

She tried to brush him aside with her hand but he retaliated in the most frightening way. The Genie transformed himself into a hideous, four-legged creature with warty, reptilian skin and a barrel chest. The drooling beast had vicious teeth and eyes that smouldered like fire. It was like a hideous, nightmarish dog.

'Rooooooooooooar!!!!'

'Oh no!' said Janine, knocked backwards across the floor.

The suction cables were dropped and quite useless now.

'You were warned!' snarled the creature. 'Now you'll *pay*!'

Crouching down, the animal sprang into the air with its jaws open wide. Janine was at its mercy.

'Rooooooooooooar!'

It never landed on its victim. Three particle beams zapped the creature where they converged, halting him in mid-air where he writhed and twisted. He was imprisoned in the ball of neutron energy.

'Snaaaaaaaaarl!'

Janine looked back to see the Ghostbusters behind her.

'OK, boss,' said Peter. 'We got him!'

'Connect the cables!' urged Egon.

'Then we'll get the rest of them,' hoped Winston.

Janine did not need to be told twice.

Grabbing the two fallen cables, she lunged at the lamp and fixed the suction cups to each side. Winston lifted a small walkie-talkie set to his mouth.

'Hit it, Ray!'

Back in the car, Ray Stantz took the message.

'Roger!'

He was in the rear of the vehicle with all his ecto-traps wired together. He pressed a switch and the traps snapped open, emitting a brilliant glare of concentrated energy.

The glowing streak of energy snaked along the cables and into the house. There was a massive explosion of colours, a cataclysmic upheaval that caused the whole building to leap off its foundations. It dropped back into place.

The reversal worked!

Tons of accumulated litter blew out of the front door in a steady stream and scores of ghosts came hurtling back through the sky from all directions, to be funnelled back into the house down the chimneys and the ventilation shafts.

They screeched and howled their protests, but in vain. They went surging back *into* the lamp. The four-legged creature still struggled to get away from captivity.

'OK, guys,' said Peter. 'Time to slam-dunk this geek back where he came from.'

They shut off their beams and the suction force of the lamp did the rest, yanking the beast back into the mainstream of the spirits in an instant. The rushing sound continued until the last of the spirits was sucked safely back to its own dimension. Then the lamp imploded and dropped through a smoking hole in the desk.

'Look at my desk!' cried Janine. 'Oh, that Genie . . .!'

'He won't trouble you again,' promised Egon.

The spell had broken. Egon was himself again.

'Egon,' she said, puzzled. 'Don't you think I'm beautiful when I'm mad?'

He turned to Winston to pass a confidential remark.

'I think the strain is getting to her.'

'Thank goodness!' Janine cried in delight. 'It's all over.'

Ray and Slimer came in through the door to join the others. They gathered round the brave young woman who had been their boss.

'Janine,' said Peter, 'you showed a lot of guts today.'

'Yeah,' agreed Ray. 'We'd be proud to have you as a fully-fledged Ghostbuster.'

'Glug-glug-glug!' said Slimer enthusiastically.

Janine pushed him away as he tried to kiss her.

'No sliming me, Slimer!' She turned to the others. 'Thanks. Thanks a lot, guys. But I've decided to stick with my old job.' She gave a shrug. 'I think I'll be a lot happier leaving the ghostbusting to – the Ghostbusters.'

'OK,' said Peter casually, 'you're the boss.'

'Don't say that word!' she protested.

'Easy,' he added, calming her. 'It's just a figure of speech.'

'Oh,' she said with relief.

The Ghostbusters and Slimer moved away.

'Goodnight, Janine,' said Egon.

'Goodnight, Egon.'

Left alone, she sat at her desk with her chin propped up by her hands. She let her fantasies wander again.

'If only I could have had my third wish', she sighed dreamily. 'Boy, I'd wish for . . .'

But the words died on her lips.

Slimer and the four Ghostbusters appeared from nowhere to clap their hands over her mouth. They did not want her to wish for anything.

'Shhhhhhhhhhhh!' they hissed.

Janine had had enough wishes for one day.

THE REAL GHOSTBUSTERS No. 2

GHOSTS-R-US

THE REAL GHOSTBUSTERS No. 3

SLIMER, COME HOME

by Kenneth Harper

If you enjoyed JANINE'S GENIE
you're sure to enjoy GHOSTS-R-US
and SLIMER, COME HOME.

Coming soon – to save the world!

KNIGHT BOOKS

GHOSTBUSTERS

novelisation by Larry Milne

(based on the screenplay by
Dan Aykroyd and Harold Ramis)

Who or what can deliver New York from the
dreaded tyranny of the paranormal? Who can
save the city from a plague of ghosts that will
spare no living creature and leave no street
unvisited?

Who but a half crazed trio called the Ghostbusters. Poised between genius and lunacy,
these cosmic crusaders alone have the power
to combat a force unknown to human kind . . .

CORONET

MASK

novelisation by Kenneth Harper

Welcome to the World of MASK – Mobile Armoured Strike Kommand where illusion and deception team up with man and machine.

All these books are available at your local bookshop or newsagent, or can be ordered direct from the publisher. Just tick the titles you want and fill in the form at the end.

Prices and availability subject to change without notice.

Hodder and Stoughton Paperbacks, P.O. Box 11, Falmouth, Cornwall.

Please send cheque or postal order, and allow the following for postage and packing:

U.K. – 55p for one book, plus 22p for the second book, and 14p for each additional book ordered up to a £1.75 maximum.

B.F.P.O. and EIRE – 55p for the first book, plus 22p for the second book, and 14p per copy for the next 7 books, 8p per book thereafter.

OTHER OVERSEAS CUSTOMERS – £1.00 for the first book, plus 25p per copy for each additional book.

Name ....

Address ....

....